STAND UP SPEAK OUT

RACIAL JUSTICE

Virginia Loh-Hagan

45TH PARALLEL PRESS

Published in the United States of America by Cherry Lake Publishing Group
Ann Arbor, Michigan
www.cherrylakepublishing.com

Reading Adviser: Beth Walker Gambro, MS, Ed., Reading Consultant, Yorkville, IL
Content Adviser: Kelisa Wing
Book Designer: Jen Wahi

Photo Credits: © Daniel Samray/Shutterstock.com, 4; © Roman Chazov/Shutterstock.com, 6; © LeoPatrizi/iStock.com, 8; © Grandbrothers/iStock.com, 11; © Johnny Silvercloud/Shutterstock.com, 12; © Michal Urbanek/Shutterstock.com, 14; © Fiora Watts/Shutterstock.com, 17; © grandriver/iStock.com, 18; © RozenskiP/Shutterstok.com, 20; © Christine Glade/Shutterstock.com, 23; © archna nautiyal/Shutterstock.com, 24; © F Armstrong Photography/Shutterstock.com, 26; © CatwalkPhotos/Shutterstock.com, 29; © bgrocker/Shutterstock.com, 30, additional cover images courtesy of iStock.com

45th Parallel Press is an imprint of Cherry Lake Publishing Group.

Library of Congress Cataloging-in-Publication Data

Names: Loh-Hagan, Virginia, author.
Title: Racial justice / Virginia Loh-Hagan.
Description: Ann Arbor, Michigan : Cherry Lake Publishing, [2021] | Series: Stand up, speak out | Includes index.
Identifiers: LCCN 2021004981 (print) | LCCN 2021004982 (ebook) | ISBN 9781534187528 (hardcover) | ISBN 9781534188921 (paperback) | ISBN 9781534190320 (pdf) | ISBN 9781534191723 (ebook)
Subjects: LCSH: Racial justice–Juvenile literature.
Classification: LCC HM671 .L64 2021 (print) | LCC HM671 (ebook) | DDC 323–dc23
LC record available at https://lccn.loc.gov/2021004981
LC ebook record available at https://lccn.loc.gov/2021004982

Printed in the United States of America
Corporate Graphics

About the Author:

Dr. Virginia Loh-Hagan is an author, university professor, and former classroom teacher. She's currently the Director of the Asian Pacific Islander Desi American Resource Center at San Diego State University. Her job is all about fighting for racial justice! She lives in San Diego with her very tall husband and very naughty dogs.

TABLE OF CONTENTS

Activists often work as a group. They have power in numbers.

WHAT IS RACIAL JUSTICE?

Everyone has the power to make our world a better place. A person just has to act. **Activists** fight for change. They fight for their beliefs. They see unfair things. They want to correct wrongs. They want **justice**. Justice is upholding what is right. Activists help others. They serve people and communities.

Activists care very deeply about their **causes**. Causes are principles, aims, or movements. They give rise to activism.

Many activists feel strongly about racial justice. Race refers to more than skin color. It also refers to physical and cultural identities. Historically, it's been a way to sort people into groups. Groups are treated differently. **Racism** is when people are treated unfairly because of their skin color. White people tend to have more **privilege** than others. Privilege means having power or an advantage. People of color are often **oppressed**, or abused by power.

People of color and their **allies** want racial justice. Allies are supporters. Racial justice is fair treatment of all people. It's creating fair systems. It's making sure people get equal opportunities.

In this book, we share examples of racial justice issues and actions. We also share tips for how to engage. Your activist journey starts here!

● Racial justice activists can be people from all different races.

GET STARTED

Community service is about helping others. It's about creating a kinder world. Activism goes beyond service. It's about making a fairer and more just world. It involves acting and fighting for change. Choose to be an activist!

○ **Focus on your cause!** In addition to the topics covered in this book, there are many others. Other examples include addressing economic injustices and ending job discrimination.

○ **Do your research!** Learn all you can about the cause. Learn about the history. Learn from other activists.

○ **Make a plan!** Get organized.

○ **Make it happen!** Act! There are many ways to act. Activists write letters. They write petitions. They protest. They march in the streets. They ban or boycott. Boycott means to avoid or not buy something as a protest. They perform art to make people aware. They post to social media. They fight to change laws. They organize sit-in events. They participate in demonstrations and strikes. During strikes, people protest by refusing to do something, such as work.

BLM is an international community. They help others fight anti-Black racism. They provide shared goals.

CHAPTER 1

SUPPORT BLACK LIVES MATTER

Black Lives Matter (BLM) is a movement. BLM activists fight for Black rights. They fight against racism. "Black Lives Matter" is a **rallying** cry. Rallying means the act of coming together. #BlackLivesMatter is also a social media **campaign**. Campaigns are courses of action. BLM rallies people and makes them aware of the injustices against Black people. Activists make BLM signs. They march in the streets. They protest.

Trayvon Martin was a 17-year-old Black teen. In 2012, he was walking home from a store. He was shot and killed by a neighborhood watch person. The person wasn't punished for Trayvon's murder. This made people angry. Students at more than 30 high schools in Trayvon's hometown walked out of class. They chanted, "Justice for Trayvon."

GET INSPIRED

BY PIONEERS IN RACIAL JUSTICE ACTIVISM!

○ **Sojourner Truth** fought to free enslaved people. Enslaved means forced to work for free. She helped freed Black people get jobs. In 1851, she gave a famous speech called "Ain't I A Woman?" She also fought for the rights of Black women.

○ **Emma Gee** and **Yuji Ichioka** were the first to use "Asian American" in the 1960s. The term united people of Asian heritage. It inspired Asian American activism.

○ **John Lewis** was a leader of the civil rights movement. He fought for equal rights for Black people. He marched. He made speeches. He led sit-ins. He was jailed. He was beaten. But he never quit. He became a U.S. congressman in 1986. He served until his death in 2020.

○ **Nelson Mandela** fought against the system of apartheid in South Africa. Apartheid denied rights to Black people. He led non-violent protests. He went to jail. He didn't stop fighting. In 1994, he became the first Black president of South Africa.

BLM is about love and community.

Alicia Garza is a civil rights activist. She was upset by Trayvon's murder. She wrote on social media, "I continue to be surprised at how little Black lives matter. Our lives matter." Garza, Patrisse Cullors, and Opal Tometi founded the BLM Network in 2013.

Jen Reid is a BLM protestor. She's from Bristol, England. In 2020, she and others protested to remove Edward Colston's statue in Bristol. Colston lived more than 300 years ago. He made money from the slave trade. The protestors pushed the statue into a river. Reid climbed up.

Many reading lists to support diverse voices can be found online.

She made a raised fist. A statue was made of her. Reid's statue secretly replaced Colston's statue. "BLM" was written in front of it. The city took down Reid's statue and sign. But people were still inspired.

Stand Up, Speak Out

Reading gives us knowledge. It also makes us more caring. Marley Dias is a teen activist. She started the #1000BlackGirlBooks campaign. She inspires others to read books about Black females. Activists want to amplify diverse voices. You can help!

> Start a book club. Read about people of color. Discuss what you learned. Learn about experiences different from yours.

> Support authors of color. Support diverse stories. Talk to local librarians. Ask them to buy more diverse books.

> Write to your school leaders. Write or speak to your school boards. Ask them to require schools to teach about diversity. Ask them for money to buy diverse books.

Black people are more likely to by stopped by police.

CHAPTER 2

FIGHT FOR CRIMINAL JUSTICE REFORM

Criminal justice reform is aimed at fixing the unfairness in the criminal justice system. People of color are not treated the same as White people. For example, Black people are sometimes stopped by the police for no reason. They're jailed more. They're more likely to be shot and killed by police.

Police are part of the criminal justice system. Activists want to stop police violence. Colin Kaepernick was a famous football player. In 2017, he knelt instead of standing when the national **anthem** was sung before a game. An anthem is a song representing a nation or group. Kaepernick inspired others to kneel. He protested against police violence.

GET INSPIRED

BY LEGAL VICTORIES

○ In 1868, the 14th Amendment became law. This law granted citizenship to former enslaved people. It protected the rights of Black Americans. Some southern states opposed the law. President Andrew Johnson also opposed the law. He vetoed it. Veto means to deny. But Congress overrode him. This was the first time Congress overrode a presidential veto. The 14th Amendment has been used in many court cases. It ensures every citizen should be treated the same by the government.

○ Nido Taniam was a college student from northeast India. In 2014, he was a victim of a hate crime in the city of Delhi. His father said, "It was racism . . . he was killed because of the way he looks." There were many protests. Activists pushed for more police protection. They pushed for anti-racist laws. This would be the first time India dealt with racial discrimination. Activists are still fighting.

George Floyd was a Black man. In 2020, he was unjustly killed by police. His murder was caught on video. It went viral. It sparked concerns about the mistreatment of Black people. BLM organized protests in more than 2,000 cities in more than 60 countries. Between 15 and 26 million people participated. These protests were the largest in U.S. history. Many BLM activists shouted, "**Defund** the police." Defund means to decrease money. Activists want to pay for support services instead.

The George Floyd protests began in Minneapolis, Minnesota.

The Innocence Project fights to reform the criminal justice system. They fight in courts. They help people who've been wrongly jailed. They also study the reasons why the system has failed people.

Many detention centers are at cities at the border between the United States and Mexico.

Stand Up, Speak Out

Migrants and **refugees** are people who come to the United States. Many are people of color. They're running from danger. They're treated like criminals. They're sent to **detention** centers. These places are like jails. The conditions aren't good. Families are separated. Activists want to end immigration detention. You can help!

> Write letters to people in the detention camps. Letters help people feel human. They help people feel less lonely and stressed. They show that others care.

> Learn to be an ally. Learn how to support immigrants.

> Learn how to create safe spaces for others. Host workshops. Teach others.

At first, only rich White men could vote.

CHAPTER 3

SECURE VOTING RIGHTS

Voting lets us choose our leaders. Leaders make laws and policies. Voting is the right of citizens. In the United States, activists fought for voting rights for women and people of color. Voting injustices still exist today.

The American Civil Liberties Union (ACLU) Voting Rights Project protects people of color. In 2010, there was an issue with the school board elections in Sumter County, Georgia. Voting district lines were changed. This change left out voters in the Black community. It voted in White candidates instead of Black candidates. The school district was 70 percent Black. But the school board was 70 percent White. This didn't seem fair. The ACLU sued and won. They fought to fairly include Black voters.

GET IN THE KNOW

KNOW THE HISTORY

○ **1619** A Dutch ship brought 20 enslaved Africans to Jamestown, Virginia. White European settlers used Black **labor** to make money. Labor means work. About 6 to 7 million enslaved people were stolen. They were forced to work in the North American colonies.

○ **1775** The Pennsylvania Abolition Society was formed. It was the first official U.S. organization for abolitionists. It had Black and White members.

○ **1882** White Americans were scared that Chinese immigrants were taking away their jobs. The Chinese Exclusion Act was passed. It banned Chinese immigrants from coming to the United States. Chinese American activists fought against it in courts.

○ **1933** Adolf Hitler was the leader of Germany. He supported a racial purity law. He believed tall, White, blonde, blue-eyed people were the "master race." He was the leader of the Nazi Party. They committed **genocide**. Genocide is the killing of many people from a specific group. They targeted people who didn't fit their ideals. The Nazi Party was defeated in World War II.

The 2020 election saw a historic number of Black voters.

Voter **suppression** is stopping specific people from voting. Voter **intimidation** is scaring people. It keeps people from voting the way they want. People of color are often at risk. Their voting rights are threatened.

Black Voters Matter makes sure Black votes count. They fight against suppression. They fight against intimidation. They boost voter turnout. They ensure voting access.

Jimmy Carter was the 39th president of the United States. His Carter Center ensures fair elections. It has watched over more than 100 elections in about 40 countries. Carter's agents reassure voters they can vote safely and secretly. They stop election scams. They watch the entire voting process.

Young voters have helped elect people of color and women.

Stand Up, Speak Out

U.S. citizens can't vote until they're 18 years old. Takoma Park is in Maryland. In 2013, it became the first U.S. city to let people 16 and older vote in local elections. A few other cities are doing the same. Activists are working to boost voters. They're fighting to lower the voting age. You can help!

> Learn more about Vote16USA.org. This is a national campaign. Join their email list.

> Work to change local laws. Work to change state laws.

> Write, email, or call politicians. Ask people to sign petitions.

Migrant farm workers often work long hours in uncomfortable positions.

CHAPTER 4

ABOLISH FORCED LABOR

Forced labor means making people work for free. In U.S. history, White people had enslaved Black people. This was called slavery, and the United States is still feeling the effects. Forced labor is still happening today. It hurts people of color the most. Activists fight to **abolish** forced labor. Abolish means to totally stop.

Migrant workers move from place to place. They often work on farms. They're often people of color. They often don't speak the language of power. Many are not treated well. They're not paid well. Some are not paid at all. Dolores Huerta fought for farmworkers. She hosted boycotts and strikes. She came up with the famous chant, "Sí, se puede," which means, "Yes, we can!"

GET INVOLVED

There are several groups fighting for racial justice. Connect with them to get more involved.

○ **CHOOSE** was founded by teens Winona Guo and Priya Vulchi. They want to help people talk about race. They listen to people. They share people's stories. They create guides. They write books. They make speeches. They give people tools and skills to fight racism.

○ **Know Your Rights Camp** was founded by Colin Kaepernick. The group fights for Black and Brown communities. It hosts camps for children of color. The camps teach kids about activism and their rights.

○ **The NAACP** is the National Association for the Advancement of Colored People. They've been fighting for civil rights since 1909. They want to abolish race-based discrimination.

○ **UWD** is United We Dream. They support undocumented immigrants. Undocumented means not having official papers. UWD is the largest immigrant youth-led community in the country. They provide leadership training. They fight for justice and dignity.

The Uyghurs live in northwestern China. They're a Muslim minority group. The Chinese government forced the Uyghurs into camps. They force them to work long hours. They give them little to no pay. The Uyghurs make much of the clotheing we wear. About 1 in 5 cotton clothing comes from Uyghur forced labor.

The fashion world benefits from forced labor.

Activists write letters to fashion companies. They push them to not make clothes from factories using Uyghur labor. They encourage us to not buy from these companies. Models can be activists too. Model Alliance and Free Uyghur Now are activist groups. In 2020, they protested during New York Fashion Week.

● Anyone can be an activist.

Stand Up, Speak Out

Around the world, children of color are forced to work. They usually live in **developing countries**. These countries have less income and industry than more developed countries. Their families live in **poverty**. Poverty means they have very little money. Children work in factories. They carry heavy loads. They can't go to school. They can't play. They're not treated well. Activists want to abolish child labor. You can help!

> Research what you buy. Don't buy from companies that use child labor. Write to these companies. Tell them why you're not buying from them.

> Write to politicians. Tell them to support programs and laws that abolish child labor.

> Celebrate June 12. This is the World Day Against Child Labor. Make posters. Host workshops. Teach people about the issues.

GLOSSARY

apartheid (uh-PART-hyde) a system of racial segregation in South Africa

abolish (uh-BOL-ish) to end or stop completely

activists (AK-tih-vists) people who fight for political or social change

allies (AL-eyes) supporters

anthem (AN-thuhm) a song that represents a nation or group

boycott (BOI-kot) to refuse to buy something or take part in something as a protest to force change

campaign (kam-PAYN) an organized course of action

causes (KAWZ-es) the reasons for activism

criminal justice reform (KRIM-uh-nuhl jus-TISS ree-FORM) fixing the unfairness in the justice system that widely affects people of color

defund (dee-FUHND) to decrease money for something

detention (di-TEN-shuhn) a place that holds or detains people

developing countries (di-VEL-uh-ping KUHN-trees) countries that are growing their industry

enslaved (in-SLAVD) forced to work for free

genocide (JEH-nuh-syd) the killing of many people from a specific group

intimidation (in-tih-muh-DAY-shuhn) scaring someone into doing something

justice (JUHSS-tiss) the upholding of what is fair and right

labor (LAY-buhr) work

migrants (MYE-gruhnts) people who move from place to place

oppressed (uh-PREST) being abused by power

poverty (POV-ur-tee) a state of lacking the money necessary to survive

privilege (PRIV-uh-lij) a special advantage or unearned power

racism (RAY-sih-zuhm) treating people unfairly based on their skin color

rallying (RAH-lee-ing) the act of coming together

refugees (reh-fyoo-JEES) people who have to escape from a country for fear of their lives

strikes (STRYKES) organized protests where people refuse to do something

suppression (suh-PREH-shuhn) stopping or preventing someone from doing something

LEARN MORE!

Jewell, Tiffany, and Aurelia Durand (illust.) *This Book is Anti-Racist: 20 Lessons on How to Wake Up, Take Action, and Do the Work.* London, UK: Frances Lincoln Children's Books, 2020.

Nichols, Hedreich, and Kelisa Wing. *What Is the Black Lives Matter Movement?* Ann Arbor, MI: Cherry Lake Press, 2021.

Tyner, Aritka R. *Black Lives Matter: From Hashtag to the Streets.* Minneapolis, MN: Lerner Publishing Group, 2021.

INDEX

31

The Glittering World of Gems

AWESOME OPALS

By Joyce Jeffries

Published in 2018 by
KidHaven Publishing, an Imprint of Greenhaven Publishing, LLC
353 3rd Avenue
Suite 255
New York, NY 10010

Designer: Seth Hughes
Editor: Vanessa Oswald

Photo credits: Cover (left) Stellar Gems/Shutterstock.com; cover (right) Alexander Hoffmann/ Shutterstock.com; cover, pp. 1–2, 4, 6, 8, 10, 12, 14, 16, 18, 20–21, back cover (background) ILeysen/ Shutterstock.com; p. 5 artshock/Shutterstock.com; p. 7 Fat Jackey/Shutterstock.com; p. 8 (opals) Fribus Mara/Shutterstock.com; pp. 9, 10 (tools) Ian Waldie/Getty Images; pp. 11, 20 (top, gem) Auscape/UIG via Getty Images; p. 13 mark higgins/Shutterstock.com; p. 15 hlphoto/Shutterstock.com; p. 17 Gift of Clare Le Corbeiller, 1991/Metropolitan Museum of Art; p. 19 Albert Russ/Shutterstock.com; p. 20 (top, lower portion of hand) bai1ran/iStock/Thinkstock; p. 20 (bottom) Mielon/Wikimedia Commons; p. 21 (top and bottom) DavidPlane1/Wikipedia.

Cataloging-in-Publication Data

Names: Jeffries, Joyce.
Title: Awesome opals / Joyce Jeffries.
Description: New York : KidHaven Publishing, 2018. | Series: The glittering world of gems | Includes index.
Identifiers: ISBN 9781534523104 (pbk.) | 9781534523142 (library bound) | ISBN 9781534522992 (6 pack) | ISBN 9781534523005 (ebook)
Subjects: LCSH: Opals–Juvenile literature.
Classification: LCC QE394.O7 J43 2018 | DDC 553.8'73–dc23

Printed in the United States of America

CPSIA compliance information: Batch #BS17KL: For further information contact Greenhaven Publishing LLC, New York, New York at 1-844-317-7404.

Please visit our website, www.greenhavenpublishing.com. For a free color catalog of all our high-quality books, call toll free 1-844-317-7404 or fax 1-844-317-7405.

CONTENTS

WHAT OPALS ARE MADE FROM

Opals are unique gems made from silica, which is one of the most common elements on Earth. This element is found in sand. An opal is different than most gems because it doesn't have a crystal-like **structure**.

The water content in opals is higher than it is in most gems. Sometimes an opal is called a **mineral** gel, which means it's soft. An opal can easily break because of this softness. However, this also makes it easier to shape raw opals into finished gemstones for **jewelry**.

Mining for Facts!
Opal is the birthstone for October.

A white fire opal stone is in this ring. Opals are used in jewelry of all kinds.

WHERE TO FIND OPALS

Gem-**quality** opals are very **rare**. Most of these opals are found in South Australia where the weather is hot. There are a few large opal mines in this area, but most of them are small.

The best opals are generally found in Coober Pedy, Australia. The ground in this area is soft, which makes it easy to dig through. Opals are often found near the earth's surface. Only a few people typically work in these opal mines.

Mining for Facts!

Other popular opal mining spots around the world include Brazil, Mexico, Honduras, Hungary, Indonesia, Ethiopia, and the western United States.

Shown here are open mining **shafts** in Coober Pedy, Australia.

WHAT OPALS LOOK LIKE

An opal changes colors as the stone is turned. An opal looks like a rainbow gem because it reflects more than one color of light.

Gem-quality opals come in many different colors. The most common colors of opal found in Australia are white and green. White and green opals are the least **valuable**. Black opals with red coloring are the most valuable and are very rare.

Mining for Facts!

The town of Lightning Ridge in New South Wales, Australia, is famous for its black opals.

These rough-cut black opals can be made into expensive jewelry.

8

This miner in Coober Pedy, Australia, is looking at a finished opal.

HOW TO MINE OPALS

There are a few ways to mine opals. One of the most popular methods used by miners is to dig a shaft. While digging, they carefully remove small bits of dirt and rocks until they discover what looks like rainbow-colored rocks. This is called an opal **deposit**. These rocks are then taken to be washed.

Opals are also mined by large mining businesses that use bulldozers. Although this method is more expensive, these large machines remove dirt and rocks more quickly than shaft mining. However, when miners find an opal deposit, they remove this rock with simple hand tools.

Shown here is a bulldozer digging up dirt and rocks to find opals.

FINDING OPALS

When an opal is found, it's raw and doesn't look very special. It's often mixed in with other rocks and put in a cement truck drum with water. The drum spins and washes away the dirt.

Once the dirt has been removed, miners start to sort the rocks by hand. Sometimes miners can miss opals, since gem-quality opals can be mixed in with other rocks. Miners called "noodlers" look through the waste rocks left behind, and sometimes they find leftover opals.

Mining for Facts!

In 2008, NASA discovered opal deposits on Mars.

This rock has opal deposits in it.

13

CREATING OPAL JEWELRY

Before an opal is ready to be made into jewelry, it's cut from rocks using diamond-tipped saws and a lot of water. A jeweler tries to keep as much of the opal as possible and only remove waste rock.

Jewelers work very carefully with raw opals because they're only as hard as window glass and can easily break. A raw opal often holds a lot of water, but sometimes it can dry out. When this happens, the opal becomes hard and can easily crack.

Opals come in all colors of the rainbow!

15

FINISHED OPALS

To make finished opals, jewelers go through a very careful **process**. After the raw opal is cut from the rock, jewelers shape and **polish** it to bring out its bright colors.

All opals come in a rounded cabochon shape. This is because an opal is too soft to be cut with flat surfaces. To make it easier to place an opal in a jewelry **setting**, a thin piece of darker, harder stone is attached to the back of it.

Mining for Facts!

Opal jewelry is most often put in a bezel setting, which is generally gold or silver. This setting goes around the gem to keep it safe and hold it in place.

This pendant made by French designer René-Jules Lalique has a cabochon opal.

17

AN OPAL'S VALUE

The two most important features of a gem-quality opal that increase its value are color and size.

Black opals from South Australia are very valuable and rare. These gems can appear in many different colors—from jet black to dark blue. The most common and least expensive black opals have green or blue stripes. When a black opal has red stripes, it's called a red fire opal. This kind of opal is the most expensive. Larger opals are always more valuable. These gems are measured in carats. One carat is equal to 0.007 ounce (200 mg).

Mining for Facts!
The native people of Australia called opal "Rainbow Serpent."

This very rare red fire opal was found in Hungary.

19

FAMOUS OPALS

What: Galaxy Opal, which is one of the world's largest polished opals

When: This opal was found in 1976. It was named the world's largest polished opal by *The Guinness Book of World Records* in 1992.

Where: Brazil

Weight: 3,749 carats (749.8 g)

Value: unknown

What: Tiffany Opal Necklace

When: Louis Comfort Tiffany designed this pendant necklace at the beginning of the 20th century. This necklace was donated to the Smithsonian Institution's National Museum of Natural History in 1974.

Where: The black opals in the necklace were found in Lightning Ridge, Australia.

Weight: unknown

Value: unknown

What: The Flame Queen Opal

When: found in 1914 by Jack Philips, Walter Bradley, and Joe Hegarty

Where: Lightning Ridge, New South Wales in Australia

Weight: 263 carats (52.6 g)

Value: sold at an auction in 2008 for $120,000

Mining for Facts!

The Flame Queen changes color when viewed at different angles.

21

GLOSSARY

deposit: An amount of a mineral in the ground that built up over a period of time.

jewelry: Pieces of metal, often holding gems, that are worn on the body.

mineral: A natural, solid substance that is not a plant or animal.

polish: To rub something with a soft cloth to make it smooth and shiny.

process: A series of steps to do something.

quality: The standard of something.

rare: Not seen very often.

setting: A piece of jewelry that goes around a gem to hold it in place.

shaft: A long and narrow tunnel that leads to a mine.

structure: The physical makeup of an object.

value: The worth of something.

FOR MORE INFORMATION

Websites

Gem Kids: Opal
gemkids.gia.edu/gem/opal
Visitors to this website find fun facts about opals.

National Geographic Kids: Opal
kids.nationalgeographic.com/explore/science/opal/#opal-raw.jpg
This website has cool photos of and information about opals.

Books

Callery, Sean, Gary Ombler, and Miranda Smith. *Rocks, Minerals & Gems*. New York, NY: Scholastic, 2016.

Hansen, Grace. *Gems*. Minneapolis, MN: ABDO Kids, 2016.

INDEX